BARRON'S

Reading Clubhouse

MIXING COLORS IS FUN

By Stacy Chambers

BARRON'S

Table of Contents

Illustrations on pages 5, 7, 9, 11, 13, 15, and 17 by InContext Publishing Partners

All inquiries should be addressed to:
Barron's Educational Series, Inc.
250 Wireless Boulevard
Hauppauge, New York 11788
www.barronseduc.com

Library of Congress Catalog Card No.: 2006032251

ISBN-13: 978-0-7641-3729-7
ISBN-10: 0-7641-3729-8

Library of Congress Cataloging-in-Publication Data
Chambers, Stacy.
  Mixing colors is fun / by Stacy Chambers.
      p. cm. — (Reader's clubhouse)
  ISBN-13: 978-0-7641-3729-7
  ISBN-10: 0-7641-3729-8
  1. Color in art—Juvenile literature. 2.
Painting—Technique—Juvenile literature. I. Title.

  ND1488.C44 2007
  701'.85—dc22

                                                          2006032251

PRINTED IN CHINA
9 8 7 6 5 4 3 2 1

Dear Parent and Educator,

Welcome to the Barron's Reader's Clubhouse, a series of books that provide a phonics approach to reading.

Phonics is the relationship between letters and sounds. It is a system that teaches children that letters have specific sounds. Level 1 books introduce the short-vowel sounds. Level 2 books progress to the long-vowel sounds. Level 3 books then go on to vowel combinations and words ending in "y." This progression matches how phonics is taught in many classrooms.

Mixing Colors Is Fun reviews the ending "y" with a long "e" sound, the ending "y" with a long "i" sound, and the "ue" and "ew" vowel combination sounds. Simple words with these vowel combinations are called **decodable words.** The child knows how to sound out these words because he or she has learned the sounds they include. This story also contains **high-frequency words.** These are common, everyday words that the child learns to read by sight. High-frequency words help ensure fluency and comprehension. **Challenging words** go a little beyond the reading level. The child may need help from an adult to understand these words. All words are listed by their category on page 23.

Here are some coaching and prompting statements you can use to help a young reader read *Mixing Colors Is Fun:*

- **On page 4, "new" is a decodable word. Point to the word and say:**

    Read this word. How did you know the word? What sounds did it make?
    Note: There are many opportunities to repeat the above instruction throughout the book.
- **On page 16, "statue" is a challenging word. Point to the word and say:**

    Read this word. Look at the beginning sound. How did you know the word? Did you look at the picture? How did it help?

You'll find more coaching ideas on the Reader's Clubhouse Web site: *www.barronsclubhouse.com.* Reader's Clubhouse is designed to teach and reinforce reading skills in a fun way. We hope you enjoy helping children discover their love of reading!

Sincerely,

Nancy Harris

Nancy Harris
Reading Consultant

Did you know you can make colors on your own? When you mix two colors, you always get a new color.

Every color starts with red, yellow, or blue. Choose two of those colors and mix them. You will get a new color.

Look at this green jewel. How would you paint this jewel?

Mix blue and yellow. You can paint this jewel green. What if you took away blue? What color would the jewel be?

Look at this tasty orange. How would you paint this orange?

Mix red and yellow. You will get orange. What if you took away yellow? What color would the orange be?

Look at this purple jelly. How would you paint this jelly?

Mix red and blue. You will get purple. What if you took away red? What color would the jelly be?

Look at this blue sky. How would you paint this kind of blue?

Mix blue with a little white. You
will get this kind of light blue.
What if you put in more blue?
What color would the sky be?

Look at this red cherry. How would you paint this kind of red?

Mix red with a little black. You will get this kind of red. What if you took out the black? What color would the cherry be?

Look at this gray statue. How would you paint this statue?

Mix white with a little black.
You will get gray. What if you
took away white? What color
would the statue be?

It is fun to play around with colors. Start with one color. Mix in a tiny bit of another color. Or mix in a lot.

Every time you mix, you make a new color!

Fun Facts About
COLORS

- Red, yellow, and blue are called primary colors. All other colors are made with primary colors.

- The name "primary colors" was chosen because "primary" means "first."

- Orange, green, and purple are secondary colors. They are made by mixing two primary colors. Can you guess why they are called "secondary" colors?

- Do you know how to make brown? Mix together all three primary colors.

Find Out More

Read a Book

Leonni, Leo. *A Color of His Own.* Knopf
  Books for Young Readers, 2000.

Schmitz, Diane Ridley and Kathy Howard
  (Editors). *Paint Magic (Art Magic).* North
  Light Books, 2001.

Watt, Fiona. *The Usborne Book of Art Skills
  (Art Ideas).* Usborne Books, 2003.

Visit a Web Site

The Art Room
http://www.arts.ufl.edu/art/rt_room
This fun and educational site helps you
learn to think like an artist. Learn to make
and keep your own sketchbook. Browse
the art library made just for kids. Also, kids
are able to send in their own artwork to be
displayed on the Web site!

Glossary

 **green** the color you get when you mix blue and yellow

 **jelly** mashed-up fruit that you spread on bread or other food

 **orange** the color you get when you mix red and yellow

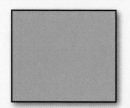 **purple** the color you get when you mix red and blue

 **statue** a figure of a person, animal, or object made of stone or some other hard material

Word List

Challenging Word

statue

Decodable Words

blue	new
cherry	sky
jelly	tasty
jewel	tiny

High-Frequency Words

a	fun	of	to
always	get	on	took
and	green	one	two
another	how	or	what
around	if	out	when
at	in	own	white
away	is	play	will
be	it	put	with
black	kind	red	would
can	know	start	yellow
color	little	the	you
colors	look	them	your
did	make	this	
every	more	those	

Index

Photo Credits:

Cover: © Emanuele Taroni/Getty Images
Page 4: © Ian Woollams/Getty Images
Page 6: © Harry Taylor/Getty Images
Page 8: © Royalty-Free/Corbis
Page 10: © Bruce Esbin-Anderson/Alamy
Page 12: © Tim McGuire/Corbis
Page 14: © Dinodia Images/Alamy
Page 16: © Rudy Sulgan/Corbis
Page 18: © Emanuele Taroni/Getty Images
Page 19: © Royalty-Free/Corbis
Page 22, top: © Medioimages/Alamy
Page 22, 2nd from top: © ImageState Royalty Free/Alamy